THE LONELY TYPEWRITER

Max and Peter dedicate this book to their parents,
who first introduced them to typewriters, Max to
a Remington and Peter to a Smith Corona.

First published in 2014 by David R. Godine, *Publisher*,
Post Office Box 450, Jaffrey, New Hampshire 03452
www.godine.com

Text copyright © 2014 by Peter Ackerman

Illustrations copyright © 2014 by Max Dalton

First printing, 2014
Printed at Toppan Leefung Printing Ltd. in China

Library of Congress Cataloging-in-Publication Data

Ackerman, Peter.
The lonely typewriter : a picture book / by Peter Ackerman ;
illustrated by Max Dalton. — First edition.
pages cm
Summary: A typewriter Pearl used to type pamphlets for Dr. Martin Luther King Jr.,
then her daughter Penelope used to write love letters to her future husband,
Paxton, has grown lonely in the attic but comes to the aid of their son, Pablo,
when the computer freezes as he tries to write a paper for school.
ISBN 978-1-56792-518-0 (alk. paper)— ISBN 1-56792-518-9
1. Typewriters — Fiction. 2. Family life — Fiction. 3. Loneliness — Fiction.
4. Computers — Fiction.] I. Dalton, Max, illustrator. II. Title.
PZ7.A18255Lot 2014
[E] — dc23
2014012058

THE LONELY TYPEWRITER

A picture book by Peter Ackerman

Illustrations by Max Dalton

David R. Godine · Publisher · Boston

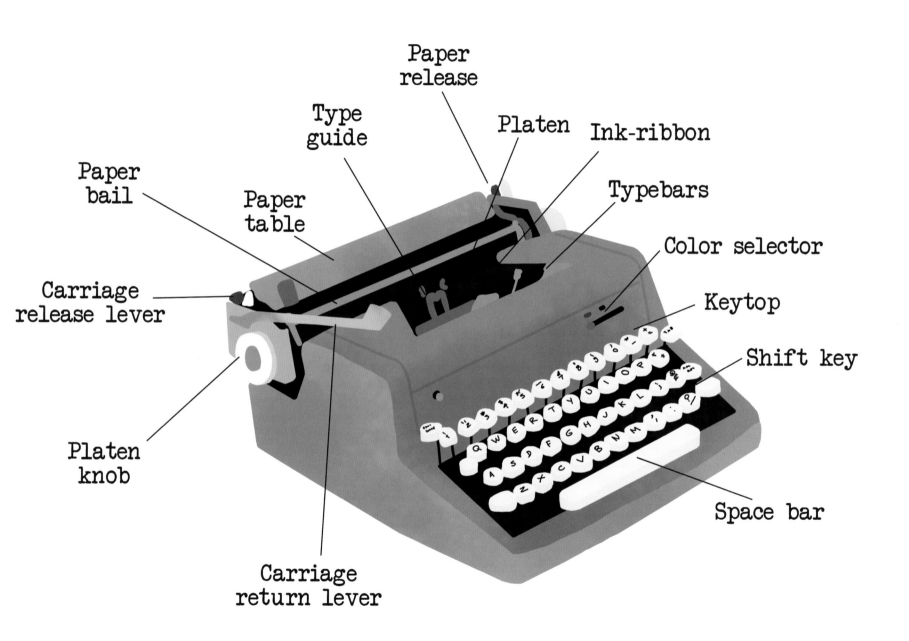

Paper release

Type guide

Platen

Ink-ribbon

Paper bail

Paper table

Typebars

Color selector

Carriage release lever

Keytop

Shift key

Platen knob

Space bar

Carriage return lever

THE LONELY TYPEWRITER

Once upon a time there was a typewriter.

Its pale yellow keys were held up by crooked metal elbows. Its

gleaming silver arm stuck out like it wanted to shake your hand.

Its owner, a young woman named Pearl, used it to type pamphlets for Dr. Martin Luther King, Jr.

Twenty years later, her daughter, Penelope, used it to type the book that won her a poetry prize.

She even typed her first love letter to a poker player named Paxton.

The typewriter was very happy.

Then one day Penelope bought a computer.

It worked much faster than the typewriter and let Penelope fix her mistakes on the screen and look up anything she wanted to know.

9

Penelope didn't need her mom's old typewriter anymore,

so she put it up in the attic and forgot about it.

From that day on, the typewriter became lonelier...

and lonelier

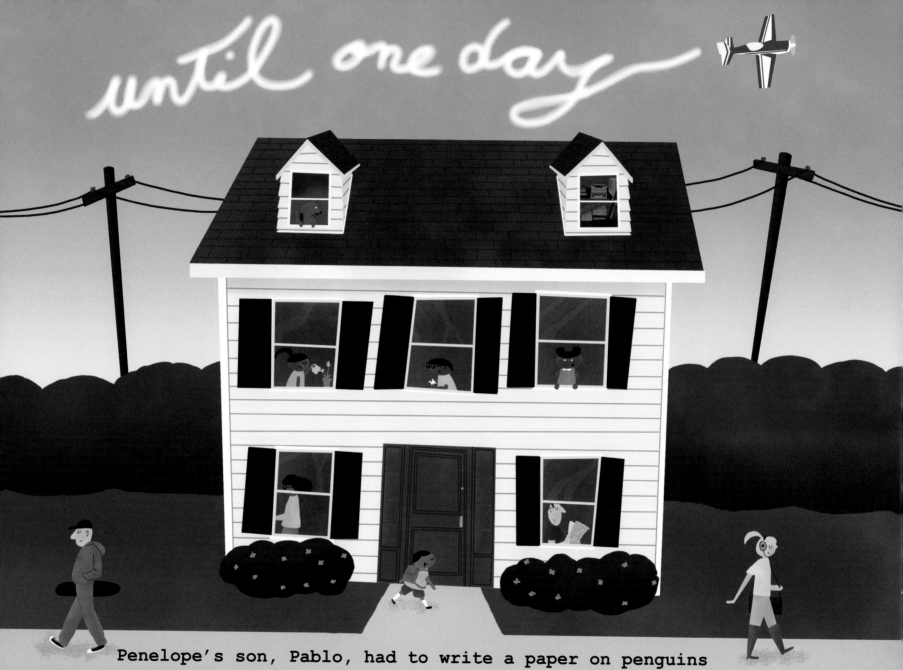

Penelope's son, Pablo, had to write a paper on penguins
for school. But he didn't want to write a paper on penguins.
He wanted to play ping-pong with his sister, Sam.

Pablo hit a forehand slice, a backhand dipsy-doodle, and a sideways scrunch.

Then his sister, Piper, asked

him to paint.

Pablo painted pirates and a

parrot named Fred, which reminded

him of his brother, Fred.

So he raced upstairs and made Fred walk the plank.

Then they all had the best pillow-fight ever.

Until their father called them down to dinner. *"Hooray!"* said Pablo. *"Taco night! My favorite!"*

For dessert they had Upside-Down Pineapple Cake, which was the *only* cake Pablo liked to eat upside-down.

When they finished, Penelope said, "Pablo, isn't
it time for you to write your paper on penguins?"
Pablo frowned, fumed, and held his breath.

"You can use my computer," said his father.

So Pablo looked up
penguins and found
out they're really
cool! In ancient times
they grew to be six
feet tall.

And they can swim fifteen miles per hour!

And dive 1,800 feet deep!

And though you would think they are cousins

to puffins, they are not. Penguins are penguins.

And puffins are puffins. Period. And...

...oh no!

The mouse froze.

The cursor wouldn't move.

The computer was broken and Paxton couldn't fix it. "What will I do?" said Pablo. "I haven't even started typing yet!"

Penelope had an idea.

Up in the attic, under dust and spiderwebs, sat
the typewriter. Its pale yellow keys stood alert
like soldiers. Its long, silver arm stuck out
like it wanted to shake Pablo's hand.

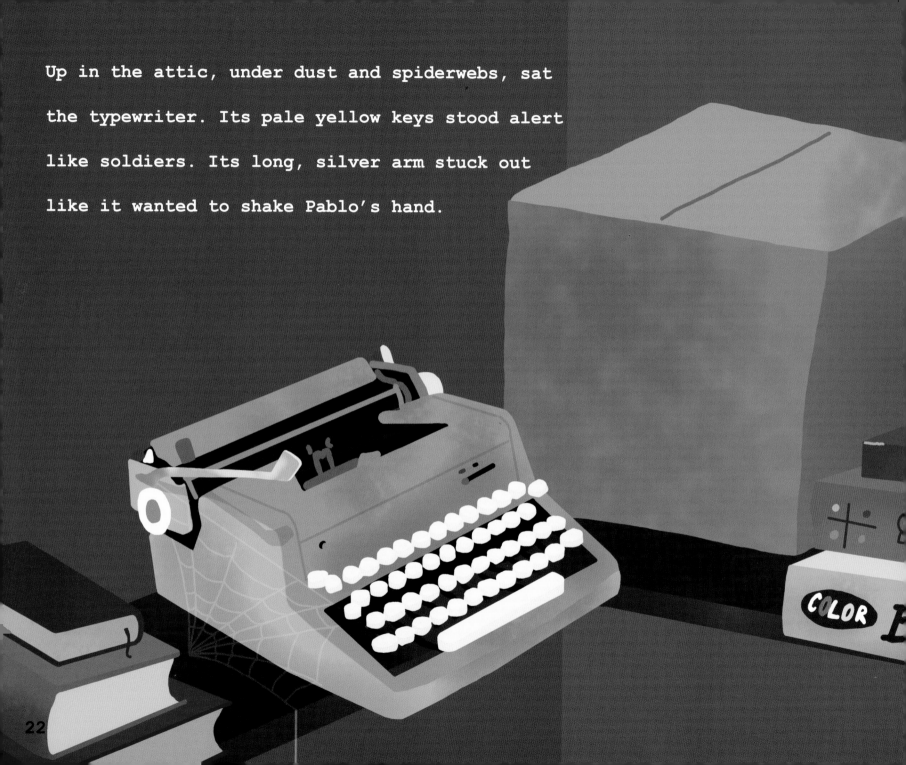

"What's that?" asked Pablo.

"A typewriter," said his mom.

"A what-writer?"

"A typewriter. It's what we used before computers."

"Before computers?!" gasped Pablo. "Where is the screen?"

"Nowhere."

"Where do you plug it in?"

"Nowhere."

"What kind of batteries does it use?"

"None."

"Then how does it work?"

Penelope carried the type-writer to Pablo's desk. She took a blank piece of paper, set it behind the black tube, and turned the knob.

CRAANNK!

The typewriter sounded like someone who had been sitting in a corner for twenty years and finally got to stretch his back. "Aaahh," said Penelope. "I remember this."

Pablo gently pressed the P key. A skinny metal bar kicked up but did not

touch the paper. "Harder,"said Penelope. "Like this." She pressed sharply —

THWACK! — stamping a P on the page!

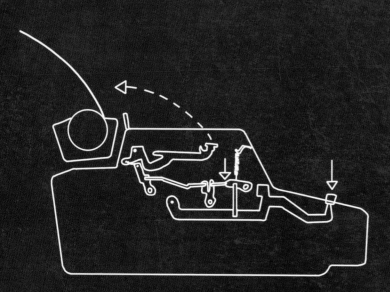

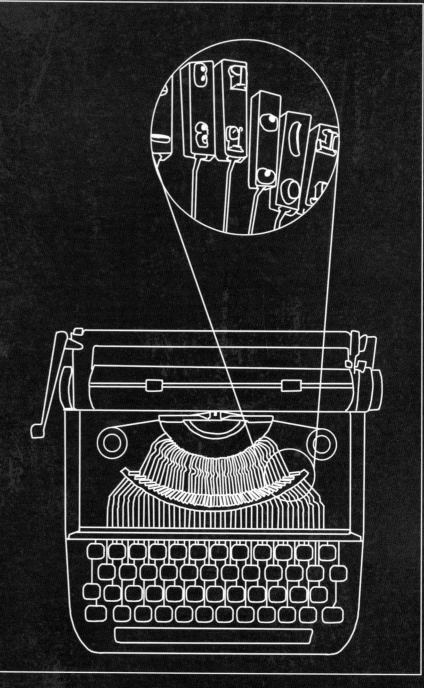

"How did *that* happen?" asked

Pablo. "The P on the typebar is

raised," she said. "When you

thwack it against the ink in the

ribbon, it marks the page."

"Cool!" said Pablo. "But it looks crooked."

"That's something I always loved about this typewriter," said Penelope.

"It has personality. When I sent letters to your dad, he always knew

they were from me." Pablo reset the paper and thwacked out...

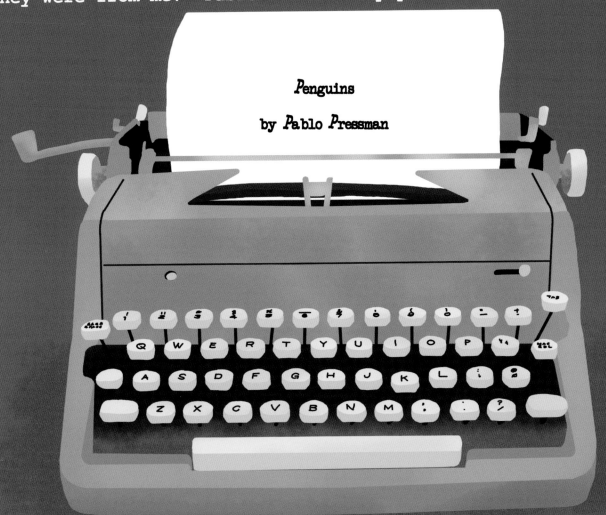

Penguins

by Pablo Pressman

It was hard work, but Pablo kept at it: clack-clack-clack, ding! Craannk! His family came running in to see what was making all the racket.

"Is the P still crooked?" asked Paxton.

Penelope smiled.

28

The next day, fingers still tingling, Pablo handed in his paper to his teacher, Mrs. Peppenpooper. "Wait a minute," she gasped. "Did you type this on a *typewriter?*"

"A *what-writer?*" asked the kids.

"A *typewriter,*" said Pablo. "It doesn't need a screen or electricity or anything! It was my grandma's and then my mom's and now I get to use it. We had it stuck up in the attic, but now I'm going to keep it in my room with me."

And, for the first time in a
very long time indeed, the
typewriter was lonely no more.

The End

The End

Other Books by Peter Ackerman and Max Dalton

The Lonely Phone Booth

Other Books by Max Dalton

Extreme Opposites